BOOT IT!

I am a reader and I celebrated
World Book Day 2023 with this gift
from my local bookseller and
Old Barn Books

**OTHER BOOKS BY
A. M. DASSU**

BOY, EVERYWHERE

FIGHT BACK

BOOT IT!

by A. M. Dassu

AN OLD BARN BOOK

First published in the UK by Old Barn Books Ltd 2023

Copyright © A. M. Dassu 2023

Old Barn Books Ltd
West Sussex
RH20 1JW

Old Barn Books is an independent publisher of picture
books, and fiction for people aged 9+.

Follow us on Facebook, Instagram or Twitter @oldbarnbooks
Email: info@oldbarnbooks.com
Web: www.oldbarnbooks.com
Distributed in the UK by Bounce Sales and Marketing Ltd
Sales@bouncemarketing.co.uk
ISBN: 9781910646830
Cover illustration by Zainab 'Daby' Faidhi
Typesetting and design by Sheila Smallwood
Printed and bound by CPI Group (UK) Ltd, Croydon, CR0 4YY
1 3 5 7 9 10 8 6 4 2

WORLD BOOK DAY®

World Book Day's mission is to offer every child and young person the opportunity to read and love books by giving you the chance to have a book of your own.

To find out more, and for fun activities including the monthly World Book Day Book Club, video stories and book recommendations, visit **worldbookday.com**

World Book Day is a charity sponsored by National Book Tokens.

For everyone who felt they couldn't achieve their dream because they didn't belong

— A. M. Dassu

Chapter 1
ALI

'Come on!' I shouted, looking back at Sami as we raced down the corridor towards the sports hall. Sami's shoes clobbered the tiles as he came up close behind me, panting.

'Ali, wait! Have you got your pen?' he asked. 'Mine's in my bag outside the lunch hall.'

'Uhh… yeah.' I slowed down to feel around in my blazer pocket.

A few spaces had come up on the football team because some year eights had moved school in the Easter holidays. Mr Clarke was talking about 'refreshing' the line-up before the Under 13's County Cup coming up in May, so we'd played football at the park every day in the holidays to get ready for the trials. Sami was so fast at dribbling, it was hard to keep up with him. We'd taken turns to man-mark each other and were both really good at it now. We'd practised taking loads of penalties against Mark, our best goalie, hoping we'd all get picked to play for the school. It was finally our time to shine. And I couldn't *wait*.

'Let's go to the park after school again today, yeah?' I said to Sami as we approached the notice board outside the sports hall. 'I've looked up some more drills to try on YouTube.'

'Which ones? I thought we'd covered everything.'

'Found some for receiving the ball on the back foot,' I said, watching Sami gawp at the board.

We'd run all this way because we thought we'd be the first to write our names down, but there were already two on the list:

1. Nathan (CAPTAIN)

Of course that dimwit got there first and was assuming he'd be captain again...

2. Tom

Hmmmm… they were good players. And they'd been on the team since year seven.

If Mr Clarke chose us all, we'd just have to try and get on and focus on winning for the school.

'Here.' I handed my pen to Sami after I'd put my name on the list and pulled out the pizza slice I'd wrapped in a napkin from my pocket. The cheese had melted and stuck to the napkin and, as I pulled the slice out, the cheese came off with it too. Oops.

Sami looked at the pizza as if he was going to gag.

'What?' I shrugged. 'You're the one who wanted to get your name on the list so bad! What was I meant to do, put the pizza in my pocket bare?'

'Ugh! Stop it!'

We both laughed as he put my pen to the paper pinned on the notice board and I took a big bite of pizza... with no cheese.

Sami al-Hafez, he wrote in his curly-wurly, super-neat handwriting. It was straight, even on a wall. I don't know how he wrote things so neat, but he always did.

We both grinned when he'd finished. 'Hey, add Mark's name too,' I said, remembering he'd messaged me from the dentist to make sure I didn't forget.

'Mark S-mi-th,' said Sami as he wrote Mark's name. 'Shame Aadam can't join us.' 'Yeah, if he could, he'd definitely make the team!' Aadam was like Sami's older bro, even though they weren't really brothers. If he had the refugee paperwork that Sami had and was just a bit younger, we were pretty sure he'd be scouted to play in an academy in the Premier League. He was *that* good.

I turned to see Elijah coming towards us with his pencil case in his hands. He'd added a neat line through his buzz cut, like Drake. I wondered when he'd done that—it looked fresh.

He's good at football, I thought as we passed him, nodding at each other.

'So, what you doing after park footy?' asked Sami, handing me my pen.

'Nothin'. Come and play FIFA at mine?' I put my pen in my pocket.

'I can't. Sara's got some open classroom thing and I have to go too. She's settled into her new school really well and Mum said we all have to show our support and go and ooh and aaah over her books.' He rolled his eyes.

'Ah, okay. Yeah, you gotta go to that then,' I said.

'Yeah, got no choice. It's her first school thing in England and Mum and Dad are acting like it's the event of the year.' He smirked at me. 'She's playing a lobster in her school play, hasn't even got a speaking part—obviously—but Dad's just so happy she's going around snapping us with her pretend pincers and playing with everyone again. She's going to show me her lobster mask or whatever she's made today 'cos I'll miss the play because of school.' He sighed and shoved his hands into his trouser pockets with a faraway look.

Was he still feeling guilty? Sami had told me his sister stopped speaking because she was in a mall that got bombed and it was 'cos she'd gone with his mum to get him some football boots. It wasn't *his* fault they'd had to leave Syria, but I think he still thought it was. I knew I'd better distract him before it got him down again.

'You still gonna be at the park, though?' I said, pulling open the door into the lunch-hall corridor, where our bags were.

'Nah, I can't be late for Sara's open classroom thingy. Mum and Dad will be waiting for me.'

Sami grabbed my rucksack from the shelves outside the hall and handed it to me, then grabbed his. I wiped the grease off my hand with the non-cheesy side of the napkin and slung my rucksack over my shoulder.

My phone buzzed, so I pulled it out of my trouser pocket. It was Mark. He'd sent a message with a photo of a sticker.

Man got himself a big boy sticker from the dentist :D

'Look at this.' I showed Sami and he

laughed.

'What you doing?' I asked, as Sami started searching through his rucksack and pulled a textbook out.

'My pencil case. It's not in here.'

'Did you leave it in last lesson?' I said, as we headed outside.

'I dunno. I'll go check,' he said, zipping his bag up. 'Meet you on the field?'

'Yeah, see you there.'

'Hey, Ali!' shouted Sami outside French, across the mob of kids in the corridor. 'Let's go see who else is trying out before we head home!'

'Yeah, go on then.' I shoved my hands in my pockets and followed him. The crowd of kids squeezed around us, rushing to get out of the school doors as if there was a fire.

The sports corridor was empty, but we could hear people in the changing rooms, getting ready for their after-school clubs.

'That's weird,' said Sami, pointing at the try-outs list. His brow creased as he got closer to read the names.

'What's weird?' I said, catching up to him.

'My name has a line through it.'

'What?' I nudged his shoulder and stood beside him staring at the list. Now, with Sami's name crossed off, there were ten names. Mine was still at number three, untouched. Mark's was still number five. 'You think it was Nathan?' I said.

'Nah, probably just a mistake,' said Sami, trying to look as if he wasn't bothered, when it was obvious he was. He grabbed a pen from the front compartment of his rucksack and rewrote his name on the twelfth line.

'There,' he said, smiling. 'We've got our team now.'

'Yeah, let's just hope Mr Clarke thinks so.' I glanced at the extra sheet pinned below the one with our names on it. 'I bet more people will have signed up for the trials by tomorrow, though.'

'Oh look, the team kit list!' Sami moved over to read it.

His bag dropped on the floor.

I looked at the rucksack lying next to my shoes and then at him. His face was as pale as my mum's unfried samosas. I picked up his bag and tried to hand it to him but he was dazed.

What the heebie-jeebies had he seen?

Chapter 2
SAMI

'I'm not coming to the trials,' I announced at lunch the next day, over the noise of scraping chairs and clanging cutlery.

Ali pulled his loaded fork out of his mouth. 'Bro, what?'

'Look.' I shoved the team kit checklist I'd printed earlier in the library in front of his face.

My heart started racing again and I

tried to block the image of the bombed-out mall forming in my head. If I hadn't begged Mama to go to the mall and get me new boots for the school football trials back in Syria, Sara would still be talking and we'd never have had to leave.

'What's the list got to do with you coming to the trial?' Ali asked.

'I need proper boots... I thought I could just play in my normal trainers. And I'm not asking my mum or dad to get football boots after what happened last time!'

'Oh, right,' Ali said, dropping his fork on his plate.

'Why can't I just play in the trainers I've got? I'm good in them when we practise!'

'Mate, just wear my boots from last year! They don't fit my little brother yet, so they're just sitting in the downstairs shoe cupboard wasting away.'

Ali looked so relaxed about it all. I knew I'd be letting him down big time if I didn't go to the trials. It was all he'd talked about throughout the Easter holidays. This was his first chance to try out for the school football team because he was sick at the start of year eight and missed out, and he'd started year seven mid-year. I couldn't ruin this for him. And, I guess, football made me feel alive and like I had a purpose in England.

But, since seeing the kit list, I kept thinking about what had happened to my family because of me. I'd even had a nightmare... my first in months.

'Just come round to mine after school and try them on, yeah?'

I sighed and picked up my burger.

Ali stared at me, his brow creased. 'Sami, it's not the same as last time. You know you're safe now. And no one is gonna bomb the mall in England that we aren't sending anyone to… I've got the boots at home, man.'

I knew he was right. If I didn't make Mama go and buy me a pair of new boots, it wasn't the same as last time. At least I hoped.

'Oof.' I pushed my left foot into Ali's old boots in the changing room, looking around to check if anyone could see me struggling to get them on. I could imagine Nathan making a Cinderella's ugly sister joke or something, but all the boys were distracted, pulling on their shirts and boots. Excitement buzzed through the air and it felt as if I could touch it.

The boots were tight, but I'd made up my mind. I was going to play in them the best I could. There was no way I'd ask Mama or Baba for new ones in my size. If I didn't ask, then nothing bad would happen. And I might even get on the team. If I made it, I'd WhatsApp Joseph first thing. We'd both be playing for our school team… even if we were on different continents.

Mr Clarke put his head into the changing room. 'Come on, boys. Let's get started.' He smiled at us and closed the door again.

Ali hung his backpack on the peg, zipping it up. He put his fist out to me and then to Mark, who was changing next to him. 'Let's do this.'

'Let's go!' Mark put his fist out too

and I bumped them both.

I ran on to the pitch behind Ali and Mark, my boots pinching my toes. *You only have to have them on for half an hour,* I told myself as I took my place across the pitch from Ali. Mr Clarke put me and Ali on the same team as forwards, and Mark on the other team in goal. Mark didn't look happy. He pushed his curly blond hair off his face and ran to join Nathan, who was announcing who would be taking corners and acting like he was definitely going to be captain again.

When Mr Clarke blew the whistle, I focused. Tom kicked off and the ball made it to the midfielders; they dodged tackles from the other team and Elijah kicked it towards me. I ran up and took the pass, taking a breath. It was just me and the ball… and Ali. We'd practised so much, I knew exactly what he was going to do with the ball and where I had to go next. I locked eyes with Ali and he nodded at me. This. Was. It. Our one chance to make the team.

I dribbled the ball, passing Mr Clarke standing on the sidelines. I wondered if he was impressed by my ball control, but I couldn't risk glancing up at his face and losing my focus. I dribbled round Nathan's legs and passed back to Ali. He weaved through the other team, moving fast towards their goal. I raced into position. 'Ali! Over here!'

Nathan was coming for him, and just as Nathan went for the ball with a sliding tackle, Ali crossed it to me and I tapped it past Mark, into the net. YESSSSS!

'AAAGH!' Nathan shouted, putting both his hands on his head.

I bent over, panting with exhaustion.

'Get back into your positions!' shouted

Mr Clarke.

After twenty more minutes of play, Mr Clarke blew his whistle.

'Well done, boys!' I looked up to see that Mr Clarke was grinning. He walked over with his clipboard and I straightened up, wiping the sweat from my face with my shirt.

Ali was sitting on the grass, out of breath, watching Mr Clarke as if he was about to give out a prize.

'You were great,' Mr Clarke looked at me, Ali and Tom, who was stood behind us.

'When do we find out if we made it, Sir?' I thought I'd better check.

'I'll put the team list on the notice board tomorrow morning.' He smiled and turned towards the school building.

'Do you think we might actually get on the team?' I asked Ali as he got up.

'I hope so, man! It would be messed up if we don't. We did good!' Ali said. 'Come on, let's get changed.'

I covered my nose as I entered the changing room, trying to mask the smell of sweat and stinky shoes that was wafting towards us.

'Here, you might need this.' Nathan threw a banana at Elijah. *'Ooh-ooh, ah-ah!'*

Ali put his hand on my arm.

I froze.

Elijah slammed the banana on the bench and grabbed his towel.

'Come on, do the noise,' Nathan said, nudging Tom, who was next to him. Tom didn't say anything, so Nathan shoved him. 'Go on! Do it!'

Tom hung his top on a peg and looked at Nathan, then mumbled the sound.

Elijah sucked his teeth and left for the

showers with his head down, while Nathan roared with laughter as if he'd made the best joke in the world.

'Louder, come on!' Nathan shoved Tom harder.

'OOH-OOH, AH-AH!' Tom shouted. Like a puppet on strings.

Apparently they were neighbours as well as best mates. I shuddered, thinking about not being able to get away from Nathan in school and then at home too.

Nathan jumped from foot to foot. He was beaming, having the time of his life, until he saw us and his face straightened.

He pushed his chest out. 'You two can't change here – you smell of curry and it makes me feel sick,' he said, turning to laugh with the boys changing beside him. His brown hair was stuck to his forehead with sweat and he looked even more twisted than when he'd egged me in the toilets and called me a terrorist on my first day at school.

Ali gave me the death stare as if to say, 'Ignore him.'

'You weren't too bothered when you were picking up your curry takeaway from Khan's restaurant, were ya?' shouted Mark from behind us.

'OOOOOOH!' all the boys in the changing room roared.

Nathan balled up his fists, his ears glowing hot pink as if they belonged to someone else's face, but didn't say anything more. He turned to pull clothes out of his sports bag.

Good. Because we had better things to do. We finally had something to look forward to – tomorrow we'd find out if we'd be playing for the school team. And if we were, that was going to be awesome.

Chapter 3
ALI

'We got in, man!' Mark fist-bumped me and Sami *again* as we entered the park after school the next day.

'Yeahhh, we did!' I shouted while ripping off my blazer and running to the far side. I dropped it to make a goalpost and then pulled my boot bag out of my rucksack.

Mark dumped his bag to make the other goalpost and joined me on the spongy grass while Sami sat opposite us and pulled my old football boots out of his rucksack. He added another plaster to the blister on the back of his foot before squeezing his eyes shut and scraping his heel into the boot.

'My foot's in,' he said, looking across. 'Worst bit's over.'

I nodded. If his blister was covered, he'd be able to play. Now we had to focus. Our first match was next week and we were in the park after school to get some extra practice in.

Sami ran across the makeshift pitch and stopped in front of the football.

'Try chipping it!' I said, getting up and jogging towards him while Mark stood in goal.

'Where you kick the ball up in an arc?' he asked.

'Yeah.' I got ready to take a shot after him.

'English is so funny. I wanna eat chips now!' Sami grinned, walking backwards, then ran up again and struck the ball so hard it flew across the grass, miles away from our goal.

Someone laughed out loud. I spun round to see a blonde girl, probably our age, doubling over laughing. She straightened up. 'You know you have to angle your toes down and use the top of your foot where your laces are to chip the ball, right?'

Sami's cheeks turned pink. 'New boots,' he said, looking down at his feet. 'Getting used to them.'

'Ah, okay. Can I join you?'

Sami turned to me and then to Mark in goal. He looked as stunned as I felt. What was she gonna do?

She unzipped her hoodie and dropped it on the grass, revealing a fitted red and white Arsenal shirt with 'Scott' on the back.

'Who's Scott? That you?' said Mark. He'd run up to the middle of our pitch and was standing next to me with his hands on his hips, grinning.

'There's no one called Scott in the Arsenal team,' I said, scrunching my face. I was sure there wasn't.

The girl ran to the hedge where the ball had landed, grabbed it and brought it back to us.

'Errr, actually, there is,' she said staring at me. 'Alex Scott. She plays for Arsenal *Ladies*. She's got a bunch of England caps and even played in the Olympics. She's awesome.' Her eyes sparkled as she pointed at her top. 'She's just raised money for two football pitches in a refugee camp in Iraq and I won her *actual shirt* in a competition!'

Sami raised his eyebrows. I think he was impressed by this Alex woman helping refugees in Iraq. I'd have to Google her.

'I'm Grace,' she said, nodding at us.

We all just stared at her.

'Come on, then,' she said, looking at me.

I'd lost my voice and my head. I had no idea what to do or say. What did she mean, 'come on then'? She wanted me to play *her*? Eh?

Grace dribbled the ball about a metre away and looked at me as if to say, 'Try and tackle me'.

I glanced at Sami, then Mark and

shrugged. Whatever. It wasn't as if anyone else was looking. I'd play a girl, sure.

Mark ran off to get in goal and I went for the ball, but Grace swept it away and ran with it so fast, I just stopped. Staring.

Sami raced over to get the ball from her and she weaved around him as if her legs were powered by magic. She took the ball to about three metres from the goal and stopped. Sami ran up from the side, wincing with each step, trying again to take it from her. She grinned at Sami, so confident, and chipped the ball right over Mark's head and straight into goal.

Perfectly done.

I stood with my hands on my hips, unsure how to react. Congratulate her? Hang my head in shame? What?

She didn't give me the chance.

'Looks like you boys have got a bit

more work to do.' She flicked her hair from her shoulder as if she was in one of those L'Oreal adverts my sister watched on repeat and swaggered off.

Sami cleared his throat. 'Who does she think she is?' he said.

'Good?' I said.

'A sign from heaven?' said Mark, with *OOH I LIKE HER* written all over his face.

'Yeah, a sign that we've got work to do!' I laughed. 'Come on, let's go again. Mark, leave the goal open and we'll both mark Sami, then we'll switch after a bit.'

We all ran to get in position. Boy or girl, there was no way I was going to let anyone show us up like that again.

Chapter 4
SAMI

Running on to the pitch in my school kit after a week of training sessions was unreal. It was something I'd dreamed and talked about for years and now I was actually on a school football team like I'd always wanted to be... *and* in Manchester, home of Manchester United!

Looking around, I inhaled the smell of freshly cut grass and pushed my chest out. The sun was beaming and so was I. I'd finally found my place in the UK and maybe, just maybe, I would play for Man U one day. If I managed that, I'd have enough money to go back and rebuild Syria too. Two dreams from one.

Ali ran past me and took his place. I glanced at him. I knew what I had to do; we'd talked about it enough.

Nathan slapped my back as he passed me and I almost fell over. 'Do your best, terrorist,' he said, looking back and grinning.

My toes pinched in my boots and my heel throbbed, so I ignored him. *It's just one match,* I told myself. And then I wouldn't wear Ali's boots again till that nasty blister had healed. I ran down the pitch and stood parallel to Ali.

As Mark ran out of the school building, he glanced at the sidelines and waved at someone. I turned to see it was Ali's mum. She was holding a tub of something and gesturing him over.

'Ali!' she shouted, waving a samosa at him.

Ali clocked his mum and his cheeks went red. He dipped his head and acted as if he didn't know her. I almost burst out laughing, but when he gave me a look I bent over and pretended to sort out my lace. I just knew Ali was going to flip afterwards about her turning up at our first match. I was so glad Mama and Baba were at work and hadn't come.

I stood tall after pretend-lacing-up and spotted the girl from the park. It couldn't be!

I squinted to make sure I wasn't imagining it. And I wasn't. It was her!

Grace, that was her name. The girl who had showed us up. And this was when no one else was looking. But now we were in front of the whole team and their mates and mums in the audience. Oh, man.

Our Director of Sport, Mrs Hack, went and stood next to Grace and put her arm around her. Huh? Did they know each other?

Mark ran past, shoving a samosa in his shorts pocket. The smell of fried pastry wafting from him made my stomach gurgle. I hadn't eaten anything all day in case I was sick. I'd been nauseous about the match since last night.

'She's the Director's daughter! Mad, innit?' he said.

No way! I did a double-take, catching Grace and Mrs Hack together again. How was that even possible? That meant

Grace was someone important. And it also meant she might tell her mum we were trash!

The first half flew by and before we knew it, Mr Clarke was blowing the whistle to start the second half.

Nathan kicked off.

We were 1–0 down and determined to win. Ali took the ball and eyed Elijah before passing it to him. Elijah looked at me and I ran towards the goal. The crowd was cheering and I knew this was it. My moment. I ran like I'd never run on the pitch before. The blister on my heel rubbed against the back of my boot. Again. And again. And again. And just as I was about to receive Elijah's cross, I felt a sharp pain where the blister was. Oof! It must've popped.

A wave of nausea went through me

and I tried to move differently to avoid any more damage to my foot, but that slowed me down. The other team's defender snatched up the ball and ran with it. Oh man. I clutched my heel. It felt like the skin had ripped off my foot. I gulped, tears welling in my eyes. In my biggest moment, I'd lost the ball to the other team.

'YOU IDIOT!'

It was Nathan. Ugh.

Mr Clarke shouted something and the referee blew his whistle and came over.

'Leo, take Sami's place,' Mr Clarke said. 'Sami, I'll get the nurse to see you on the bench.'

I hobbled off the pitch, my head down, my cheeks burning, trying to hold back the tears of shame brimming in my eyes. I didn't want to see Ali or Mark's face. But I knew I had to get these boots off.

I walked past the bench where I was supposed to wait for the nurse and went straight to the changing room. I'd messed up on our first match against another school. Mr Clarke might not even let me stay on the team any more. I might as well forget ever having a chance to play for Manchester United.

Nathan walked in to the changing room, sour-faced. Tom muttered 'loser' in my direction and even Leo looked at me funny. He'd never done that before. I looked down at my socks. The school nurse had cleaned up my blister and put some antiseptic cream and a dressing on my foot, while I winced and gritted my teeth. It still throbbed with pain but it felt better than it had.

'What happened, man?' Ali rushed over.

'Was it your foot?' asked Mark, staring at my heel.

'Yeah,' I said. 'I'm sorry I messed up. I couldn't carry on 'cos of the pain.' I looked down. 'I'm gonna need your help getting home.'

'Yeah, 'course. We'll just go shower quickly, yeah?' said Ali, grabbing his towel from his sports bag.

I watched them go out, wondering how I'd get my school shoes on when Nathan strode over and stopped in front of me, his legs wide and chin out.

'Why you still here?' he said with his eyes narrowed. 'You don't belong in this country, we all know that. And the only reason Mr Clarke let you on the team was because he felt sorry for you because you're a "poor homeless refugee".' He said the last part with his hands in speech marks.

I swallowed. He was probably right. And that hurt even more than my stupid blister.

Chapter 5
SAMI

'Sami, you're very quiet,' said Mama that night as she put a dish full of steaming rice on the mat on the floor. She looked up at me on the sofa and handed me a clean plate.

I took it, but didn't slide on to the floor since I couldn't sit comfortably with my blister, and we still didn't have a dining table.

'Is it your foot, or did something happen at school?' she asked.

I inhaled the smell of cloves and chicken wafting up from the dish on the mat. I didn't have anything to say. I couldn't tell her it was the football boots. I couldn't tell her I needed new ones and if I didn't get them I'd probably never play football. Not that she'd care. Mama and Baba had laughed when I'd told them I wanted to play for Man U to make my millions before I became an engineer. Baba said I had a better chance of going back to a safe and prosperous Syria than that.

Mama stared at me before pushing herself off the floor and heading back into the kitchen.

'So, what is it? You look like the world has ended,' she said to me as she returned with a tray full of empty glasses and a water jug. 'Sara, put that teddy away and eat your food!'

Sara hugged her teddy tighter.

'It's nothing. I'm fine. I don't feel well… I want to go to bed,' I said. That was true. At least I could think about what a loser I was in my bedroom in peace before Aadam and Dad got home.

I got up, handing Mama my empty plate and hobbled upstairs.

My school iPad buzzed as I got to my bedroom. I pulled it out of my backpack. Ali was video-calling me.

'What's up? Why you not replying to my messages?' he said as soon as I answered.

Here we go again, I thought.

'Did you ask your mum and dad for new boots?'

'What's the point of asking when I'm not good enough?' I muttered.

'Eh?' Ali leaned in closer to the screen. 'What d'you say?'

'Nothing.' I lay on my pillow and raised the iPad above my face so he could see me. There was no point in talking about it.

'Listen, yeah…' said Ali. 'It's not your fault you got injured. It happens *all* the time. You watch live games with me, you know that!'

He watched my face for a moment. I closed my eyes.

'You picking me up for school tomorrow?'

'Yeah…' I looked at him and could see he was worried so I sat up. 'I'm okay, it's just my foot.'

'Get your dad to look at it, yeah? He might be able to prescribe some good medicine or something.'

'Okay,' I said, even though I didn't want Baba to see it. Maybe this blister was a sign that football wasn't for me. Maybe I just wasn't supposed to play. First the football boots in Syria and now in Manchester too.

There was a long silence. I could tell Ali was stumped for words and I owed it to him to talk. 'What did your mum say? Was she annoyed we didn't have her samosas before we played?' I said, forcing myself to grin.

'Oh, man! I can't believe she brought samosas to the match to "power us up"! And Mark's shorts are all greasy 'cos the doofus put one in his pocket.'

We both burst out laughing.

'Well, I'm glad that made you laugh! Just make sure you don't get cornered by my mum and ruin *your* shorts!' Ali snorted and I grinned.

Aadam walked through the door. 'Sami, you okay?' he said.

I turned the iPad to face the door so

Ali could see him.

'Salaam, bro!' said Ali.

'Ali! Akhi! My bro.' Aadam smiled. 'What your school done to Sami?' he said, in broken English. He was getting better by the day since he'd made it to Manchester, but sometimes he'd leave out a word here or there.

'He'll be all right, mate! I'll let you go, Sami. Chat t'you tomorrow, yeah?'

'See you at eight,' I said. Ali ended the call and I put my iPad down.

'What happened? Your mum's worried about you,' Aadam said in Arabic, sitting down on my mattress next to me.

'That nasty blister on my foot popped at the worst moment. I messed up in the match, man. You'd have been embarrassed to be seen with me if you'd seen how bad I was.'

Aadam shook his head. 'You've just

got to get back out there as soon as it's healed and show them how good you are. Don't let this get you down,' he said. 'It's a shame I finish work so late that I can't join you guys in the park for practice any more.'

I put my iPad on the floor next to my mattress and sat up. 'I know, it sucks.'

Aadam smiled and tilted his head as if to say, 'Yeah it sucks because I'm so good.' He just knew it. 'Your dad wants to see you. Come, let's go down and eat.' He got up and walked to the door.

'Okay, gimme a minute.' I pushed myself on to my feet and my sock rubbed against the dressing on my heel. I hobbled forward, reminded of the shame I felt in the changing room. Nathan was right, I hadn't been put on the team because I had skills. Mr Clarke probably just felt sorry for me. I didn't belong on the team, just as I didn't belong in the UK.

I'd made my mind up. I wasn't going to play for the school football team any more. I didn't need people feeling sorry for me because I was a 'poor refugee'. I was only making a fool of myself.

Chapter 6
ALI

'Where's Sami?' I asked Mark. I pulled my phone out of the front compartment of my rucksack and messaged Sami for the fifth time. He'd missed the whole of after-school training, where Mr Clarke had us working on our speed and attacking skills, and he hadn't replied to any of my messages since our call yesterday.

'I dunno.' Mark shrugged before shoving his sweaty football shirt on a peg in the changing room. 'He's not been online and hasn't checked the group chat, but Leo said he saw him walking out the school gate.'

'He's gone *home?*' I said, putting my phone down on the bench in front of me. 'Maybe it's 'cos of his foot.'

'Yeah, probably. He can't exactly play if his blister hasn't healed.' Mark pulled out his towel and headed to the showers.

I sat on the bench and started unlacing my football boots.

Tom and Nathan burst in through the door, laughing. Nathan's face hardened as soon as he locked eyes with me.

'Why you even here? You need to go, like your terrorist mate. We don't need any useless brownies on the team.' He spat at me and his phlegm landed next to my boot, just missing it.

I clenched my jaw and bunched up my fists.

'Tell him, Tom.' Nathan nudged Tom. 'He needs to hear it from you as well.'

Tom went red. 'Yeah, we don't,' he muttered, as if he hoped no one could hear him.

But I'd heard it.

There was a silence. As if everyone in the changing room was uncomfortable but didn't know what to say.

And I couldn't blame them. I didn't know what to say or do either. Thump him with all these witnesses around and risk getting kicked off the team? Think of a comeback? Report him to the teacher and watch Nathan deny it, just like he always did? My mind went blank, so I forced myself to unravel my fists, then I grabbed my bag and clothes and stormed out of the changing room.

At dinner, I messaged Mark telling him I left without him because I had to get away from Nathan's sick face before I thumped it, and then started scrolling aimlessly through my Snapchat feed. Nathan had uploaded a story the night before, so I swiped up and saw it was a photo of our team playing at training the other day.

My chin fell and my stomach dived.

He'd put a banana emoji next to Elijah's mouth and a masked smell emoji next to me! I couldn't believe it. THE RACIST CRUDHEAD!

I'd only followed him because he'd said he'd share photos and videos of the team with his followers, but if this was his idiotic idea of supporting the team, then there was no way I was going to carry on following him.

I swiped right to the chat screen and pressed 'Remove Friend'.

There, he only had 279 followers now. One less to brag about.

'Here.' Mum put my food in front of me and sat next to me with her plate. Grilled chicken and chips, my fave. Maybe she knew I was upset today.

'Thanks, Mum,' I said, taking the ketchup bottle from her and putting my phone face down on the table before tucking in. If Mum saw the photo, she'd be straight into the school office like a firework. And I didn't want to discuss it or think about it through dinner. Why would anyone think that was an okay thing to do? I mean, I knew Nathan was an idiot, I just hadn't realised how low he could go.

After I'd put my plate in the sink and

washed my hands, I headed to the front room with my phone. My Snapchat app was still open but I couldn't see Nathan's story any more. It'd disappeared because I'd removed him. Oh man, why didn't I take a screenshot before dinner?

Instead, I saw a post about racism in sport. As if my phone knew what I'd just seen in Nathan's photo. It showed a girl standing in front of a football pitch with a sign saying:

KICK OUT RACISM AND ABUSE IN FOOTBALL

www.kickitout.org

How did my phone know what I was *thinking?* I hadn't even said anything about it out loud!

I Googled the website and saw that

it was a campaign all about encouraging people to take action and fight discrimination in football. *That's* what I needed to do.

I knew I had to stamp this out. Boot it hard like a football. There was no way Nathan could dictate who stayed on the team and who didn't, or judge us because of our colour or background. There was no way he should be able to take his nasty, racist attitude to any other team he played for. I belonged on that team as much as him or anyone else. Football was about skill, not race. I was going to report him. Maybe even report him on Kick It Out.

I swiped to our chat and video-called Sami.

Sami came over earlier than usual the next morning but it seemed like he wasn't in any mood to talk about football.

'Look, Sami,' I said, offering him a slice of buttered toast from my plate. 'Even if you don't wanna play any more, you've got to come and tell Mr Clarke what Nathan said to you. Nathan can't get away with this bull, man.'

Sami sat on the sofa with his toast, slouching, looking sick, as if I was making him eat Nathan or something. I had to convince him we had to do this together.

'Help me out, man. It'll be much better if you're with me. I'll tell Mr Clarke what he did if you want. You just stand with me. You've got more power than you think.'

Sami swallowed some toast. 'Okay… but this is just to make sure he doesn't speak to anyone else like this again, yeah? I'm not playing football any more.'

'Yeah, whatever man. We'll talk about that later. Let's go.' I tapped him on the arm. 'We've got to get to school before everyone else gets in.' I ran out the room to grab my blazer.

Mr Clarke would definitely sort Nathan out and I didn't want to say it to anyone, but maybe even demote him from being captain. That would be epic.

We walked through the quiet playground, squinting in the bright sun, and headed towards the sports department, hoping Mr Clarke would be in the office and not in the staff room.

The door to the sports hall was unlocked so we both stepped into the badly lit corridor. My eyes adjusted and took in the notice boards lining the walls.

'I'm not saying anything,' said Sami, his hands nervously gripping his rucksack strap. 'You do the talking.'

'Don't worry, I will.' I focused on the tiles ahead. 'I've known Nathan longer than you, so I can give him as much info as he wants.'

We stopped outside the office door, and stared at the sign:

SPORTS

The Director of Sport's office was next door, but she had just started her job, so I wasn't going to bother going there. Better to take this to Mr Clarke, who knew Nathan.

'Go on then,' said Sami, nudging me. 'We haven't got all day.'

'Okay, okay!' I said and knocked on the door three times.

After a few seconds, Mrs Webster, my PE teacher from year seven, opened the door wearing the school hoodie and shorts. 'Hello, boys,' she said.

'Uhhh… Miss… is Mr Clarke here?'

'Yes… You want to speak to him?'

'Uhhh, yes please,' I said, trying my best not to shuffle my feet and look awkward.

She shut the door and I locked eyes with Sami. His face said it all. He looked as nervous as I felt. My palms were sweaty and I wiped them on my school trousers. Why were we worried when we'd done nothing wrong?

Mr Clarke walked through the door and we stepped back to let him into the corridor. 'You're in early. How can I help you?' He stared at Sami. 'Are you feeling better today, Sami? Ali said you'd hurt your foot. We need to talk about—'

'Umm, Sir,' I butted in, before this became about Sami not coming to training. 'We're here to tell you about what Nathan said to us in the changing room after the match and yesterday at training.'

'What's he done now?' Mr Clarke smiled and then noticed our faces and straightened his.

'He told Sami he only got on the team because he's a refugee and you felt sorry for him…' I stopped as Mr Clarke's mobile started ringing and he pulled it out of his shorts pocket. Mr Clarke looked up at me as if to say he was listening, so I continued. 'And he said Sami doesn't belong on the team, and then he told me there were enough "brownies" on the team and I should leave too.'

'Oh, boys will be boys!' Mr Clarke looked back at his phone. 'Sorry, I've got to take this call,' he said. 'It's just banter. He doesn't mean any harm. Just ignore him! You're both great players, you know that!' Mr Clarke smiled, put his phone to his ear and went back into his office.

I looked at Sami.

'So, he's not gonna do anything?' said Sami, looking confused. 'Is that it?'

'I dunno,' I said, nudging him to walk out to the playground. 'But if he isn't, then we have to take a stand and *make* him listen.'

'Yeah, and how are we gonna do that?' said Sami, his chin almost touching his chest. This was the most deflated I'd seen him since that first week when he'd started at our school.

'I don't know, but I'm not letting Nathan get away with this. Let's think of a plan with Mark at break. Maybe even ask Elijah. We have to go big.'

'Are you gonna go to training tomorrow?' Sami asked, pushing the door open and heading out into the blinding morning sun.

'Yeah, and so are you.' I swatted a fly off my face. 'We can't let Nathan think he's beaten us.'

Chapter 7
SAMI

A few days had passed since we'd spoken to Mr Clarke and we'd had the weekend to forget about Nathan. I was at Ali's after school when his phone buzzed on the sofa. He paused the game, put his PlayStation controller on his lap and picked up his phone.

'YESSS!' he shouted, reading a message.

'What is it?' I leaned in to peek at the screen.

'My sis has just got some football boots from her friend at uni!' He showed me his phone.

'Yeah, and?' I looked at him, hung my controller between my legs and frowned.

'She's bringing 'em over now... for you, dummy!'

'I don't need them,' I said, looking down and thumbing my controller.

'Listen, these boots are definitely your size.'

I didn't say anything. Football boots and me just didn't work. Football and me didn't work.

'Look, there's no shame in borrowing boots, man. Most people can't afford new kicks every year, it's normal. I know you were used to having new things in Syria, but it's okay, man.'

'I don't care about borrowing things!

I've had to wear loads of hand-me-downs since we got here. It's not that.' I couldn't hide the frustration from my face.

'Then what is it? Your dad's special ointment's worked and your blister's healed. What's stopping you now?'

'I... I don't wanna... Look, Nathan's right. I don't belong on the team and only got in 'cos Mr Clarke felt sorry for me. I'm not gonna make a fool of myself pretending I'm good enough to be on it. I don't need anyone's pity.'

Ali put his phone on the sofa and squatted on the floor in front of me so he could see my face. 'Sami, you *are* good! Nathan is chatting bull... Listen, they can say we're too brown. They can say we don't belong. But we do. And the only way we're gonna prove it to 'em is by showing up and smashing it.' He got up and walked across the room. 'I mean, it sucks that we question our skills and we've got to work even harder to prove we're worthy of being on the team, but, Sami' – Ali turned to look at me – 'the team needs you, man, and we gotta show 'em that. Nathan can't say nothin' if it's obvious the team needs us.'

I looked straight at Ali. His eyes gleamed from the light streaming in through the net curtains. 'He won't stop, you know.'

'Well, we have to stop him. This is our dream; it's all we've talked about and we can't let him ruin it for us.'

Man, he could talk anyone into anything.

Ali squatted in front of me again. 'Just start coming to the park again for our practice sessions, yeah?'

'Okay, okay, I will. But let's finish this

game first.' I pointed at the TV with my controller and grinned. 'Let me show you my skills right here, right now.'

The next day, Elijah met me, Ali and Mark at the park after school. We'd decided we would sharpen our skills together and support each other. Our own little team. And playing together like this felt so powerful.

'Grab as many stones as you can,' Ali said, picking one up from the path. He'd made us a circuit, using paper cups he'd brought from home, with a stone on top of each one to stop them from flying off in the wind.

I picked up a stone, and then another.

'This is genius,' said Elijah, putting a stone on top of one of the cups. 'Listen, I told Leo about all this. He said he wants to come practise with us too. That okay?'

'Yeah, if he wants!' Ali said, moving a few metres to the next cup.

'It's gonna be much better practising in peace away from Nathan, man. He absolutely does my head in,' Elijah added.

'Yeah, yours and mine,' I said.

'And mine,' Ali and Mark said together.

Elijah laughed.

We started off weaving the ball quickly around the cups, trying to make it through the circuit in ten seconds. I was moving a lot better in my new boots and already feeling sharper than last week. And, man, was I relieved I'd come to practice again. It was like a heavy grey cloud had lifted from me. Thank God.

But I still wasn't sure about turning up to school training. Ali kept saying it was the only way I'd get picked for the next match, but now I just wasn't sure if I was really good enough or whether Mr Clarke was just picking me to be kind. I knew Nathan had got into my head, and for some reason, I couldn't push him out.

The next match was going to be the biggest of the term. Our school against Stockport Stepping. Our all-time rivals, apparently. We had to win this or we'd lose our winning streak against them and risk them abusing us on the buses to school. We'd also be out of the County Cup and *they'd* be through. And that would be BAD.

'Hey!'

We all stopped in our tracks and turned to see Grace running up to us. She was in a football kit, holding a PE bag.

'Can I join you? My training just got

cancelled last minute.'

'Sure,' said Ali.

'Yeahhh!' Mark said, grinning.

'Do you play for a team?' I tried to read the logo on her top.

'Oh, yeah.' Grace looked down at her logo. 'We've got a girls' football team at our school… I'm hoping your school will have one too when my mum settles in properly.' She smiled.

She's a badass, I thought, remembering how she'd played when we'd first met her. Not that I'd admit it to the boys. Whenever I'd talked about football back in Syria, Mama would go on about Sara trying out to play in the Syrian women's football league when she was older, but I'd never seen a girl play like *that* before. Leila, my friend in my old class in Damascus, would never have come near a football at school. So this was new, but cool.

'Here, you can kick off.' Mark gave the ball to Grace, his cheeks bright pink.

Grace took the ball and did a couple of keepie-uppies. 'I've got an idea,' she said. 'Can I rearrange these cups?'

'What you thinking?' said Ali, scratching his chin.

'We could do the "give and go" drill, but in a set area?'

I was trying to figure out what she meant when I heard a familiar laugh. My insides went cold.

'What… you playin' with girls now?' It was Nathan, bent over laughing exaggeratedly as if he was in a comedy sketch. 'Sounds about right. That's the perfect skill level for you idiots!' He sucked the last of his ice lolly and chucked the stick at us before walking off towards a girl who was waiting for him further down the park.

'What an idiot!' Grace shouted after Nathan, so he'd hear.

'He's always like that, ignore him. We do,' said Elijah.

'No!' Grace's face was milkshake pink against her blonde hair. 'He needs sorting out. You have to stand up to him.' Her eyes sparkled with fury. 'It's people like him that ruin the game.'

She was right. He was ruining the game. Not just for me, but for everyone.

Ali put his hand on my shoulder after our practice session. 'See, it was those old boots! You see how awesome you are?'

'I feel so good when I play, man!' I panted, smiling.

He grinned, genuinely happy for me. My bro.

'I know you've got this, man,' he said. 'No one else on the team can weave a ball so close to the goal without getting tackled. After this, if you don't wanna play on the team, I won't say a word. And if Mr Clarke picks you for the Stockport Stepping match, do it for you, yeah? You deserve to be on that pitch.'

'Don't worry, I've made up my mind. I'm coming to training and if I'm picked, I'm gonna play. For us.' I fist-bumped Ali and he breathed out. 'I had a long chat with Aadam as well last night and I agree with you guys. Nathan's opinion of us is useless. About as useless as his racist brain.'

'Yeahhh, now you got it,' Ali said.

Chapter 8
ALI

'Who's gonna win?' shouted Nathan in the changing room before the match.

'WE ARE!' everyone shouted.

He high-fived everyone… but missed me, Sami and Elijah out.

All the 'brownies'.

We'd show him.

We followed him out into the play-ground, but instead of running on to the pitch, Sami, Mark, Elijah and me got into a huddle to big each other up.

'Come on, freaks!' shouted Nathan.

We all looked at him but stayed in our huddle. We'd agreed we wouldn't let him bring us down.

'Get on the pitch!' He pointed and gestured at us, but we shook our heads. *That's* when his face went cold. He couldn't handle that we weren't listening to him.

I tried not to laugh when Sami elbowed me to get a reaction. But I was looking forward to seeing Nathan squirm.

'Let's do this!' said Sami getting out of the huddle.

I fist-bumped everyone. 'Let's go!'

Sami ran up with me and we took our positions.

Once both teams were ready, the referee blew his whistle. Tom kicked the ball to Elijah, who sent it to Leo, who then passed it back to Nathan. Sami had already found himself some space, and I could see Nathan had clocked this, but instead of driving the ball forward, he tapped it back to Leo like he couldn't be bothered to play. Nathan was making a point – he'd rather miss the chance of an early goal than pass it to Sami. I blew out in frustration.

I looked over at Mr Clarke. He had his hands on his hips and his face was scrunched up. He was obviously annoyed with Nathan too.

Sami was waving his arms furiously and calling to Leo, determined to take hold of the ball. Leo sent it to him and Sami weaved it around the player marking him. Meanwhile, I'd spotted a gap and headed straight for it. Sami knew exactly what I was doing. We were in sync again. I took the ball from my bro and took my chance, booting it hard towards the top right corner of the net.

GOALLLLL!

Me and Sami had scored! It was only because of him I got to take that shot. We ran up to each other and slammed our chests together, my heart beating so hard I could feel it. Elijah jumped on us, cheering.

Someone wolf-whistled and I clocked Grace. She'd turned up again to support us. Nice. She smiled then looked down to goal and waved at Mark. The referee blew his whistle. I breathed out. We had a long way to go before the final one sounded.

The weather had turned by half-time and the rain was pelting down on us, making it hard to see, let alone run. The other team had scored twice, so we were now drawing 2–2.

Nathan was red-faced. I'd never seen him so stressed. He'd avoided passing the ball to me, Sami or Elijah and the rage in him was spreading beyond us now, affecting his own play. After a Stockport Stepping player managed to nutmeg him, he clearly couldn't handle the shame of letting the ball through his legs and ran after the player, shoving him hard. The boy flew across the wet pitch, dramatically skidding and rolling on to his back. The referee blew his whistle and everyone jostled to see what was happening.

Mr Clarke yelled at Nathan from the sidelines to come over for a word, rubbing his brow as if he had a headache. Nathan looked panicked.

When play resumed after half-time, our team seemed to have lost all spirit. Several passes had been missed and when a pass from Tom to Sami was intercepted before Sami could get a touch, Nathan lost it.

'Just give up now, terrorist! GO HOME!' Nathan shouted at Sami.

'Okay, you know what… I've had enough!' shouted Sami, throwing his hands in the air.

'Yeah, me too!' said Elijah running towards Sami.

I looked to Mark who nodded and ran out of goal. 'And me!'

'*You* go home!' I said to Nathan, standing with my boys.

A cheer went up from the other team as the ball found the back of our empty net.

Nathan glanced across and sprinted over and kicked the ball from the goal line back into the net, hard.

Mr Clarke ran on to the pitch. 'What's happened? Mark, why have you left the goal?' His brow was furrowed, his lips straight.

We had to stand strong, even if Mr Clarke was angry with us.

'Because we've had enough,' said Sami.

'Of what?' We all turned to see Mrs Hack wearing the school-branded water-proof coat, her hood tightened around her face to keep the rain out. She'd over-heard! YESSS!

'You dirty brown idiots, why'd you do that?' Nathan yelled, storming back from goal, wiping the rain from his eyes. He stopped dead when he realised who else had joined us.

'This. We did it because of this.' Elijah pointed at Nathan.

Nathan's jaw dropped. Mr Clarke's too.

Mark stepped in between us all. 'We're not playing any more because of the way he thinks he can speak to Ali, Elijah and Sami.'

'What has he been saying?' Mrs Hack stood tall next to Nathan, while he looked at his boots. Maybe he knew his time was up.

'He says I don't belong in this team because I'm a refugee and that I'm a terrorist,' said Sami.

'He high-fived the whole team, except us "brownies" before the match,' I added. And that's his word for us, not mine. And I can't even repeat what he's said to Elijah in the changing rooms before. It's that bad.'

Elijah nodded at me.

Mrs Hack looked at Elijah, Sami and me and Nathan carried on looking at the ground.

'I see,' she said. 'So you'd rather dismiss someone's talents because of the colour of their skin and where they're from?' She looked down at Nathan as if he was chewing gum stuck to the bottom of her shoe. 'You're not going to make it far in sport then, are you, Nathan?'

'Listen boys, we have a game to finish,' said Mr Clarke checking his watch. 'We can deal with this later!'

'Yes, you have a game to finish…' said Mrs Hack.

Sami locked eyes with me. What? They were letting him get away with it, even though they'd *heard* him?

'… without a captain,' added Mrs Hack. 'Nathan, you're coming with me.'

Nathan jerked his head up, his face turning red. 'But I didn't do nothing! Tom, back me up!'

Tom shrugged. 'Think we'll play on without you. Just go.' He kept his head down and focused on his hands.

Nathan looked as if he'd been punched in the stomach. Wounded.

'You, over there,' said Mrs Hack to Nathan, pointing to the sidelines. Then, to us, 'Boys, you're doing great. Finish this game on a high – go!' She smiled at all of us then turned to Mr Clarke with a cold, hardened expression. 'Mr Clarke, see me in my office after the match please.'

Mr Clarke nodded.

The other team had circled ours, trying to figure out what was happening. Mr Clarke called one of the subs from the bench and walked off towards the referee.

Mrs Hack took a step in Nathan's direction, then stopped and turned to us. 'I wish you boys had told someone about this before. It's completely unacceptable…'

'We did,' I said.

'Yeah, we did,' said Sami, his eyes wide.

'Who did you speak to?' asked Mrs Hack.

'Mr Clarke, Miss. But when we told him about the way Nathan speaks to us, he said it was just banter.'

'Banter?' Mrs Hack did not look happy.

The referee blew his whistle to get us back in position.

Mrs Hack gestured Nathan over. He strolled back, trying not to look bothered. He really was the biggest crudhead.

'Give me your captain's armband,' she said, pointing at it.

Nathan reluctantly pulled the band down his arm. I'd never seen him look so worried.

'Here you go, Sami,' she said, handing the armband to him.

Sami beamed. He was so ready.

Chapter 9
ALI

The Stockport Stepping players leaped onto each other's backs, celebrating their win. Our year eight team was the first to lose to them in years. We lost on penalties though, after we'd managed to level the score at 3–3, so it didn't suck as much as it would've if we hadn't got our third goal.

Nathan was forced to watch Sami playing as captain. He couldn't have had a worse punishment, and Sami couldn't have had a better reward. I was loving it.

We all gathered at the side of the pitch, patting each other's backs and saying well done. Nathan stepped into our circle, pushing his soaking hair off his face before turning to look behind him. Ah, Mrs Hack. He was checking where she was.

'You lost us the game, you idiots.' He stared at Sami. 'And take my armband off. I don't want it smelling of curry.'

'Stop your nastiness and say sorry first.' Sami pulled his shoulders back and my heart swelled. He was really standing up to Nathan.

'And make sure you and none of the rest of the team make a racist or anti-refugee comment again,' I added.

'Yeah, that ain't happening, you kebab,' said Nathan, rolling his eyes and turning away. As if it just wasn't important. Mrs Hack had obviously not told him off enough.

'You know what?' Tom was standing taller now. 'You're ruining the game… for all of us. Just stop it. No one finds it funny.'

Nathan stared at him, unable to compute what was happening.

To be honest, neither could I. Were his mates standing up to him? I mean, I knew Tom had just moved house and wasn't Nathan's neighbour any more, but I didn't think he'd move on from Nathan too. Nice one.

Leo came and stood next to Tom. 'I think Sami makes a better captain, actually – maybe you should step down if you can't handle a team that looks different to you.'

'Now this is what teamwork should be. Looking after each other. Well done, boys.' It was Mrs Hack. Oh, she had a good way of being at the right place at the right time. She stopped in front of Nathan. 'If you can't ensure a safe environment for your team and that every player is treated with respect, then it seems we need to find a new captain. Leadership is a privilege. These boys are right.'

Sami and I locked eyes. *Now* we were talking!

Nathan's pink face went grey.

'We can't have anyone on the team who makes others feel worthless. We've just discussed this and yet you're refusing to say sorry, even now?'

My insides relaxed. Thank God she didn't agree with Mr Clarke. I should've gone to her all along!

'Uhhh… I-I didn't mean it like that,' said Nathan, his eyes wide with fear. He turned to us. 'Look, Ali, Sami, Elijah… I'm sorry. I shouldn't have said it… it's true, a-a captain shouldn't speak like that.' He turned to Mrs Hack as if no one else was around or watching. 'I really want to play football, Miss. Nothing else matters to me. I'll make sure they don't get no more grief. I promise.' He clasped his hands together, waiting for Mrs Hack to reply.

'Nathan, you and I need to talk.' She then turned to us. 'Sami, you were brilliant just now, stepping in at the last minute. I think I'll join you at your next training session. I'd like to see more of what you can do.' She smiled and Nathan gulped.

Sami elbowed me in my ribs sneakily

and I smirked at him from the side of my mouth.

'I'll see you all next week. Well done, boys. Have a good weekend. And Nathan... be in my office at eight a.m. on Monday,' Mrs Hack added before walking away.

'Bye, Miss!' Mark tapped me on the shoulder, nodding at me to follow him and Elijah. I glanced at Nathan's panicking face before turning at the sound of a wolf-whistle. I knew exactly who it was. Grace waved us over. She kicked the ball to Mark who did a couple of keepie-uppies before passing to Elijah.

'Well, that was a bit good,' I said, jogging over to join them. 'Now he knows he can't stop us.'

'He got wrecked, man' said Elijah, focusing on the ball bouncing on his thigh.

'Hey!' said Grace. 'Shall we have a five-a-side in the park?'

'That would be awesome,' Mark said immediately and grinned.

'Yeah, all right,' I said. Grace had skills. I'd have her on our team any day.

Sami smiled to say yes.

'Now?' I asked.

'Yeah!' she said. 'I'll get my girls over. Maybe we can play mixed teams?' She pulled out her phone.

'Let's get changed and head to the park, then,' I said, putting my arms around Sami and Mark.

'Think we've done enough standing up for ourselves for one day,' said Elijah, the ball tucked under his arm.

'Can I come too?' asked Tom. I hadn't noticed him walk over. He had his hands in his pockets and was shifting his feet.

'Yeah, 'course,' I said, blinking hard. Him too?

Maybe instead of tearing our team apart, Nathan's racist cruddery had done the exact opposite and brought us all together. He'd only gone and isolated *himself*.

It didn't matter that we'd been knocked out of the County Cup. It was as if something bigger had happened.

We'd booted the problem off the pitch, and it felt good.

Shortlisted for the Waterstones Children's Book Prize

Boy, Everywhere

How far would
you go to get back
home?

'gripping, uncompromising...
super-charged with the
power of empathy.'
The Guardian

A. M. Dassu

WINNER, LITTLE REBELS AWARD

Read on to learn how Sami's journey
started, in *'Boy, Everywhere'*

Chapter 1

It all started going wrong during English. It was the last lesson on Thursday before the weekend began, we'd just finished reading *To Kill a Mockingbird* and Miss Majida stood at the whiteboard going through some comprehension questions. I was scribbling them down, my head resting on my arm, when Leila tapped me on my shoulder from behind and handed me a note.

Are you coming ice-skating tomorrow?

I'd started writing back when the door flew open and Mr Abdo, our principal, burst into the room.

I shot up from my desk the second he entered and straightened my shoulders. Everyone's eyes were fixed on Mr Abdo, their faces blank.

'Pack your bags. You're all to go home,' he said, rubbing the creases on his tired, worn face. 'See you back here on Sunday morning.'

We didn't need telling twice. Everyone slapped their books shut and the room erupted into noisy chatter. My best friend Joseph turned to me and our eyes locked in confusion.

'Your parents and guardians have been called and are on their way to collect you,' Mr Abdo added, loosening the knot in his tie, his lips thin and tight, lines deepening across his brow.

'But why, Sir?' asked someone from the back of the class.

'There's been a bombing. This is not a drill, eighth grade. We need to get you all home. You know the protocol.'

A collective gasp rose from the room.

Through the sash windows, the sky was a clear blue. I couldn't see any smoke. Everything looked normal. The old orange tree stood firm in the sunlit courtyard, the gold crescent moon on top of the mosque's minaret gleamed in the distance. Behind it the red, white and black-striped flag on top of the church tower fluttered gently in the breeze, cars were hooting their horns and the newspaper seller was still shouting out to people passing by his stall.

Where had the bomb gone off? Panic prickled through me as I thought of home. I wished phones were allowed in school so I could just call to see if Mama, Baba and Sara were okay. I grabbed my bag to get my iPad, but remembered it wasn't in there. 'Joseph, get your tablet out,' I said. 'Just want to check what's happened – I left my iPad at home.'

'They won't have bombed anywhere near us, Sami. Don't worry,' said Joseph, pulling his tablet out of his bag and swiping to log in. 'What shall I type?' he asked, leaning in towards me.

'Google "bombing in Damascus".'

After a second, he pursed his lips and said, 'Nothing's coming up.' He showed me the error message – the internet was down for the second time that day.

My shoulders tensed. I quickly reminded myself that it was usually the outskirts of the city that were bombed. Most of Syria was torn apart because of the war, but no one had gotten close to Damascus.

'Your mama and baba are at work, right?' Joseph asked, his eyes focused on my forehead. I realised I was sweating and wiped the back of my arm across my face.

'Yeah, Baba's at the hospital but Mama worked from home today because Sara wasn't feeling well. They *should* be at the mall now,' I said, glancing at my Swatch. 'She's picking up my football boots before the trials.'

'Well, no one's ever bombed the centre. The government's always on high alert. Just chill, bro,' said Joseph, lightly pushing his fist into my shoulder before turning to put his tablet away.

He was right. But every time there was a bomb alert, I couldn't help worrying. *Damascus is safe,* I told myself. I took a deep breath, gathered my books, and packed them into my bag while Mr Abdo spoke to Miss Majida. She had her hand over her mouth and looked like she was about to burst into tears.

A backpack pushed past my arm, followed by another – everyone was leaving.

'They're doing you a favour, Sami. You weren't gonna pass the English test later anyway.' I turned to find George grinning at me, then pushing Joseph. 'Neither were you, sucker.'

Even at a time like this, George couldn't help being an idiot. Maybe it was his way of showing he wasn't nervous like me, but it was so annoying.

'You're the one that's gonna fail, loser,' said Joseph, sticking his face into George's.

George sneered at Joseph. 'Shut up! You're so fat, the only English letters you know are *K, F, C.*' He turned to me, raising his eyebrows and running his hands through his hair.

So dumb, I thought. George still hadn't gotten over Joseph coming from a non-English-speaking school.

The class babble and sound of scraping chairs made it hard to think of a quick response, but I had to stick up for Joseph, whose cheeks were now the colour of tomatoes. I rolled my eyes at George. 'We'll see. *K, F* and *C* are still three more letters than you know. Did you stay up all week thinking of that one?' His grin grew, so I added, 'Should I use *smaller* words to make sure you understand what I'm saying?' It wasn't the greatest comeback but I couldn't think of anything else.

George's mini fan club, which consisted of exactly two friends, tugged him away.

'Loser,' I muttered as they left.

Joseph and I joined the stream of kids leaving the classroom. Mr Abdo was now speaking to Miss Majida at the door, but she stopped talking the second I drifted towards it.

Joseph clutched his backpack, his head lowered. He was unusually quiet. Ugh. George had gotten to him again.

'You want to go to Damer's for ice cream after the trials?' I asked to cheer him up.

'Yeah, of course, man!' Joseph said, his eyes sparkling with excitement. 'Then we can go again tomorrow after ice-skating.' He grinned.

Mr Abdo marched past us. 'Hang on,' I said to Joseph and ran to catch up with him.

'Um, Sir, we're supposed to be going to football after school. Where should we wait?' I asked, wondering if Mama had collected my football boots.

He picked up his pace and strode into the classroom next door to ours and started talking to the teacher inside. I shrugged at Joseph as he caught up with me.

We rushed down the central stairway of the school behind the swarm of students and flowed into the large reception area, where our physics teacher, Miss Maria, was ushering everyone out of the side exit. I slowed down as I spotted Joseph's dad in a smart dark-grey suit, sitting on the deep-buttoned green leather sofa with his head in his hands. No one else's parents were inside, which was odd. The dark wood-panelled walls where the president's portrait hung made him look even gloomier.

'Baba?' said Joseph. His dad looked up.

'Ah, Sami, come here.' Joseph's dad

stood up and reached out to hug me first. *Weird.* I went to him, feeling awkward, and as he embraced me tightly my heart began to race.

He pressed my head against his shoulder and ruffled my hair, then released me and grabbed Joseph. I stepped back, feeling woozy from inhaling his strong aftershave.

'Right, let's get you both home,' he said in Arabic, turning from Joseph.

'But what about the football trials?' I asked. 'Our driver is bringing my boots. I have to wait for him!'

'Your baba asked me to pick you up. It's not safe to be out today.'

'But Baba!' Joseph interrupted. 'We were gonna get on the team today! This is so unfair!'

'Joseph, I already told you, it's not safe to be at the stadium.'

Joseph tutted, shoved the carved wooden door open, and walked out.

'Thank you! I'll keep you updated,' Joseph's dad shouted at the school receptionist as he followed Joseph out. I ran after him, my stomach lurching. Baba wouldn't send Joseph's dad to pick me up unless it was serious. Maybe the bombing was really bad. Baba would know because of the number of casualties coming in at the hospital.

The street outside school was a tangle of gridlocked cars and beeping horns. Cars were double parked across the sidewalk, leaving hardly any room to walk between them. The newspaper seller pushed papers and magazines into our sides as we walked past his stall, desperately trying to get them sold while the street was jammed with people. We all got into Joseph's dad's Honda CR-V and I pulled the seat belt over me slowly, looking out at all the parents frowning in their cars. Joseph glanced at me and then pulled out his tablet.

'Can't believe they dropped a bomb today of all days… I've been waiting ages for this,' he muttered under his breath.

'I know…' I said. 'I bet Avraham's on his way with my boots as well. He's probably stuck in all the traffic now.'

'What did you end up ordering?' he asked, pressing *Play* on a game.

'Can't get the Nike Magistas in Damascus. So I got the Adidas Predators.'

'Oooh, nice.' He looked out of the window and then said, 'Thanks for sticking up for me with George.' His cheeks were flushed again.

'No worries. I'd never leave you to face that thug alone.'

George and his stupid gang had bullied Joseph ever since we started middle school. They thought they could do or say anything they wanted because they were *ulad masooleen* – kids of government officials. I'd never seen Joseph look so sad or alone as that first week of middle school, and I never wanted him to feel that way again. I'd always be there for him. It had always been Sami and Joseph. And it would be for ever.

'Ignore him,' I said. 'He's just jealous of your skills – still hasn't gotten over last semester when you scored that penalty.'

Joseph smiled. 'Yeah, that was awesome. Do you think they'll rearrange the trials to next week now?'

'Yeah, probably.'

As Joseph went back to his game, I stared out the window, checking out everyone's cars. Leila's mama was in her grey Lexus RX, but I couldn't see Leila through the tinted glass. *Oh man*. I realised I'd totally forgotten to reply to her note after Mr Abdo walked in. I hoped I hadn't upset her. I'd message when I got home and tell her me and Joseph would be at the ice rink at 3 p.m. tomorrow.

It took twenty minutes to get out of the school street behind all the other cars, but when we got moving I could see the high-rise buildings were still intact, the roads were clear, traffic only building up near the checkpoints. There were a few fluffy clouds scattered in the sky. Some-thing circled the blue far away, probably a helicopter. I still couldn't see any smoke in the air. *They probably bombed the outskirts of the city,* I reassured myself again.

On the way to Joseph's neighbour-hood, a crowd of people were gathered outside a big villa, the men in smart suits and the women in dresses, some wearing headscarves. But I was more interested in the cars they were standing next to — a black Bentley and a white Rolls-Royce parked on the road. Both Joseph and I sat up to get a better look, our mouths open, practically drooling.

'Whoa. What do you think they're here for?' I asked Joseph.

'Probably a wedding... or a funeral,' he said, showing me his game score and smirking. 'I beat you, right?'

'Hey! Give me that,' I said, grabbing his tablet and pressing *Play*. We'd been doing this for weeks.

Joseph's dad parked outside their apartment building. As the car stopped on the smooth black tarmac, we heard what must've been gunshots in the distance. I always thought it sounded like rain hitting a tin roof. But it wasn't raining.

We jumped out, sheltered our heads with our arms and ran through their black front gates. We raced straight up to Joseph's bedroom, throwing our bags down next to some dried orange peel he hadn't bothered throwing away.

I sat on the end of his bed while Joseph switched on his PlayStation and small flat screen TV. 'May as well play *FIFA* if we can't play the real thing, eh?' he said, his chin jutting out because of his grumpy face.

'Yeah, may as well,' I said, wishing the trials hadn't been cancelled and that we were showing off the skills we'd been practising in the stadium instead.

There was a small knock on the door and it opened. 'Hi, you two. Do you want anything to eat?' asked Joseph's mama.

'Nah,' said Joseph, still facing the TV

screen, waiting for the game to load.

'How about you, Sami?'

'No thanks, Aunty, but can I have a drink, please?'

Joseph's mama smiled. 'Sure. What would you like? Coke?'

'Yes, thanks. Shall I call my mama to get Avraham to pick me up? He's probably waiting for me at school.'

'No!' she said quickly, in a strange high-pitched voice. 'Your baba wants you to stay for dinner. Stay there – I'll be right back with that Coke!' She pulled the door tight and left.

I bit my lip and frowned. Even Aunty was acting weird. I grabbed the remote from Joseph's hands and put it on TV mode.

'Hey! What you doing?' shouted Joseph.

'Shhh, I just wanna check the news. See why Baba got us picked up. Don't you wanna know?'

'Not really. All they'll show is more dead people.'

'Oh, come on, it'll only take a minute.'

'Go on then,' said Joseph.

I flicked through the channels one by one. Kids' cartoons, music, documentaries, news channel. My head started spinning as I read the headline flashing in red at the bottom of the screen.

DAMASCUS: CHAM CITY CENTER MALL REBEL TERRORIST BOMB ATTACK

I sat staring at the image on the screen. The once-shiny glass building was now partly rubble. The glass half of the mall was a broken grey shell and the concrete half was just barely standing. There were no windows or doors left in any of it and people in high-vis jackets rushed through the smoke, debris, and rows of police cars and ambulances. I watched but couldn't move. My ears throbbed. I could see Joseph's arms waving around next to me. Everything had slowed down, the noise from the TV and Joseph's words muffled. I tried to say something, but nothing came out.

The mall had been bombed. Mama and Sara were there. Buying *my* football boots.

COMING SOON:
KICKED OUT!

**Have the boys kicked out racism for good?
Can they keep their places on the team?**

Sami and Ali are living their best lives in Mark's new mansion... until money goes missing from the house and Aadam is under suspicion.

Kicked out, the boys vow to help Aadam. Battling unexpected challenges, a chance meeting with a celebrity footballer brings the hope of achieving a life goal.

Follow @oldbarnbooks on social media for updates including the cover reveal

Publication date: 19th October 2023

ISBN: 9781910646892

Price: £7.99

A MESSAGE FROM THE AUTHOR

Growing up I dreamed of becoming a writer, but I thought it was something I couldn't do, and it took me years to take the first step. Since then, all of my dreams and beyond have come true; my novels have won awards, I've met so many young readers, and I have been given the chance to write a World Book Day book, which is the hugest of honours! I think this means anything is possible. Don't give up on your dreams!

I want all children to see themselves in stories and so I write books that challenge stereotypes, humanise the 'other' and are full of empathy. You can find out more about them and what I'm up to on Twitter @a_reflective, Instagram @a.m.dassu or at www.amdassu.com. I hope you enjoy reading *Boot It!* and go on to enjoy a lifetime of great stories!

—A. M. Dassu 2023